A Grrr-eat New Friendship

Swim into more adventures!

PuRRMaiDS

The Scaredy Cat
The Catfish Club
Seasick Sea Horse
Search for the Mermicorn
A Star Purr-formance
Quest for Clean Water
Kittens in the Kitchen
Merry Fish-mas
Kitten Campout

MeRMiCORns

Sparkle Magic
A Friendship Problem
The Invisible Mix-Up

PuRRmaiDs

A Grrr-eat New Friendship

by Sudipta Bardhan-Quallen

illustrations by Vivien Wu

A STEPPING STONE BOOK™
Random House 🏠 New York

Text copyright © 2021 by Sudipta Bardhan-Quallen
Cover art copyright © 2021 by Andrew Farley
Interior illustrations copyright © 2021 by Vivien Wu

Visit us on the Web!
rhcbooks.com

Educators and librarians, for a variety of teaching tools, visit us at
RHTeachersLibrarians.com

Library of Congress Cataloging-in-Publication Data
Names: Bardhan-Quallen, Sudipta, author. | Wu, Vivien, illustrator.
Title: A grrr-eat new friendship / by Sudipta Bardhan-Quallen;
illustrations by Vivien Wu.
Other titles: Great new friendship
Description: First edition. | New York: Random House Children's Books, [2021] |
Series: Purrmaids; 10 | "A Stepping Stone Book." | Audience: Ages 6–9. |
Summary: Shelly is hosting new student Leeza, a grrrmaid, at her house,
but becomes jealous when Leeza seems more interested in
being friends with Coral and Angel.
Identifiers: LCCN 2020040243 (print) | LCCN 2020040244 (ebook) |
ISBN 978-0-593-30166-1 (pbk.) | ISBN 978-0-593-30167-8 (lib. bdg.) |
ISBN 978-0-593-30168-5 (ebook)
Subjects: CYAC: Mermaids—Fiction. | Cats—Fiction. | Dogs—Fiction. |
Jealousy—Fiction. | Friendship—Fiction.
Classification: LCC PZ7.B25007 Gr 2021 (print) |
LCC PZ7.B25007 (ebook) | DDC [Fic]—dc23

Printed in the United States of America
10 9 8 7 6 5 4 3 2 1
First Edition

This book has been officially leveled by using
the F&P Text Level Gradient™ Leveling System.

Random House Children's Books supports the
First Amendment and celebrates the right to read.

To the original Leeza,
who I thought didn't like me

1

On a clear night in Kittentail Cove, three purrmaids floated in front of the Lake family's house. The orange-striped kitten and the black-and-white kitten held up a sign that said WELCOME. The kitten with the white silky fur tried to see if anyone was swimming toward them.

"Do you see anything, Shelly?" asked Coral, the orange purrmaid.

Shelly shook her head. Then she smoothed her white fur with her paws. Shelly didn't like to have even a whisker out of place!

"My paws are getting tired," whined the black-and-white kitten.

"Just a little bit longer, Angel," Shelly said. "They are supposed to be here any minute."

Mr. and Mrs. Lake had invited a famous chef, Dewey Atwater, to cook a special feast at their restaurant. Chef Atwater decided to bring his daughter, Leeza, to Kittentail Cove, too. The Atwaters were planning to stay with the Lake family. Shelly, Angel, and Coral were waiting to welcome them to town.

It was always exciting when visitors came to Kittentail Cove. But the Atwaters were more special than the usual guests. Leeza Atwater was going to go to sea school with Shelly, Coral, and Angel tomorrow. Shelly's parents talked it over with Ms. Harbor so that Leeza could be a special guest in Ms. Harbor's class. Shelly couldn't wait to introduce Leeza to her classmates.

Of course, Shelly couldn't make her two best friends wait to meet Leeza when everyone else did! That's why she invited them to her house. She wanted Angel and Coral to greet Leeza as soon as she got there.

Shelly also had a surprise for her best friends. There was something about the Atwaters she hadn't told them. *Coral and Angel are going to be so excited!* she thought.

"Are you sure they're supposed to come tonight?" Angel asked.

"Yes, of course!" Shelly replied. "Just be patient!"

"You know it's hard for me to be patient!" Angel said. That was true. She was the kind of purrmaid who was always in a hurry. She couldn't wait for the next adventure, and so she tried to get to everything as quickly as possible!

Luckily, Shelly finally saw her father swimming toward them. "They're coming!" she exclaimed. She grinned and waved.

"Let's swim out to meet them!" Angel suggested.

"Great idea!" Shelly agreed.

Usually, Coral had a hard time keeping up with Angel. But now they were both being careful to swim side by side so the sign wouldn't rip.

"Slow down, Angel," Coral purred.

"I know, I know!" Angel said. She rolled her eyes.

Coral and Shelly giggled.

Suddenly, Angel and Coral stopped moving. Their eyes widened, and their mouths hung open.

"Why are you stopping?" Shelly asked.

Coral pointed. "Those aren't purr-maids," she whispered.

Shelly turned to face her friends. "No, they're not purrmaids," she said, giggling. "Did I forget to mention that? The Atwaters are grrrmaids!"

Grrrmaids were a lot like purrmaids. There was just one big difference. Instead of being cat mermaids, they were dog mermaids.

"Grrrmaids!" Angel said. "I've never met a grrrmaid!"

"Neither have I," Coral said.

"But we're about to!" Shelly added.

"Hello, girls!" Dad shouted, waving. The purrmaids floated closer. "This is Chef Atwater," Dad said, pointing to a grrrmaid with tan fur and black markings. "These girls are my daughter Shelly and her friends Angel and Coral."

"Nice to meet you," Chef Atwater said.

"That's a lovely sign!" He shook paws with each of the girls. Then he pulled the other grrrmaid closer. "I'd like to introduce you to my daughter," he said.

"Hello!" the grrrmaid said. "I'm Leeza!" She grinned and waved.

Leeza was a purr-ty puppy with short black fur. She had big dark eyes and a nice smile. She wore a blue-and-green top that matched her blue-and-green tail.

"It's paw-some to meet you!" Shelly exclaimed.

"Welcome to Kittentail Cove!" Coral added.

"Thank you," Leeza replied. "I've been nervous about coming on this trip. I've never met a purrmaid before!"

Shelly giggled. "We're not scary, I promise!"

"Well, you do have those claws," Leeza said. She winked to show she was just squidding around.

Shelly put her paw around Leeza. "I think we are going to have a great time getting to know each other," she purred. "We're going to be your best purrmaid friends in the ocean!"

2

"Let's get our guests home," Dad said. "They need to get settled. Tomorrow is a big day!"

The purrmaids and grrrmaids swam to Shelly's house. Mrs. Lake had a fin-tastic dinner waiting for them. "I've set out plates for everyone," she said. "Come sit down. I'm sure the Atwaters are hungry after their trip."

"Where should I sit, Shelly?" Leeza asked.

Shelly pulled out a chair. "How about here?" she suggested.

"Grrr-eat!" Leeza replied.

Before Shelly could sit down next to Leeza, Angel plopped into Shelly's chair. Angel didn't even seem to notice that Shelly was trying to sit there! Shelly scowled.

Coral was already sitting on Leeza's other side. So Shelly had to sit next to Angel. *That's all right,* she thought. *Angel and Coral will be going home soon. Then I can talk to Leeza all I want!*

The purrmaids started to eat all the yummy food. But the kittens still found time to ask Leeza questions.

"Do you have any brothers or sisters?" Coral asked.

Leeza nodded. "I have three older sisters," she said.

"That's a lot like me," Shelly said. She pointed to her older sisters, Tempest and Gale. "It's not easy being the youngest."

"I a-grrr-ee!" Leeza said.

"Who's your favorite singer?" Angel asked.

"I don't know if I have a favorite one.

I really like the Spice Grrr-ls," Leeza said. "And I also listen to Kelpy Sharkson."

Shelly's eyes grew wide. "I *love* Kelpy Sharkson! I even got to sing with her once!"

When it was time for dessert, Mom tapped Shelly on the shoulder. "We need your help."

Shelly nodded. They were having beach banana jelly served on mango slices. It was a recipe Shelly had invented when her class visited Coastline Farm. Beach bananas grew on land, so not many purrmaids used them in their cooking. Shelly thought that grrrmaids might not use them often, either!

Shelly arranged the mango slices on each plate. She put a small scoop of jelly on each one. Then she cut a piece of mango into the shape of a heart. That was the purr-fect finishing touch.

When everyone had a plate, Dad announced, "Dessert is served!"

Chef Atwater took one bite and grinned. "This is fin-credible!" he exclaimed. "I've never tasted anything like this!"

Dad winked at Shelly. "My daughter and her friends actually came up with this recipe," he purred.

"I could eat this fur-ever," Leeza said.

Shelly smiled. "Thank you!"

"I would never have thought to cook beach bananas like this," Chef Atwater said. "In Dogfish Bay, we barely even eat these. You have to share your recipe!"

"Of course we will," Mom replied. "We're looking forward to sharing all sorts of things about Kittentail Cove with you."

"And to learning about Dogfish Bay from you!" Dad added.

Shelly wanted to ask Leeza about her favorite desserts. But Coral and Angel were already asking Leeza about her hometown.

"Tell us about Dogfish Bay," Coral said.

"Well," Leeza replied, "our town is built on the edge of the Great Bark-ier Reef. So we share that part of the ocean with a lot of sea turtles."

"That's so cool!" Angel exclaimed. "I love sea turtles."

"There are also fourteen different types of sea snakes near us," Leeza added.

Coral's eyes grew wide. "Sea snakes? Are they scary?"

Leeza smiled. "They can be. But we know that if we leave the sea snakes alone, they will leave us alone."

Shelly waited for a chance to talk to Leeza about grrrmaid food. But Angel and Coral kept asking one question after another! She felt very frustrated. She

had wanted her best friends to be there to welcome the grrrmaids. But she didn't think that would mean they'd take over the whole conversation! She also wanted her best friends to become Leeza's best purrmaid friends. *I just thought I'd be a little more "best" than them!* she thought. After all, Leeza was *Shelly's* guest, not everyone's guest. It wasn't fair that Angel

and Coral were getting more time with Leeza than Shelly was!

It's time for Coral and Angel to leave, Shelly thought. She just had to think of a way to tell them that without hurting their feelings.

3

Everyone at the table seemed to be deep in conversation. Everyone except Shelly. And no one even noticed that she was being left out!

It sounded like her best friends were almost done asking about Dogfish Bay. Shelly would finally get a chance to talk! But then Coral purred, "I have many more questions, Leeza."

"Me too," Angel added.

Shelly loved Angel and Coral. But right then, she wanted them to go home. So she got out of her seat. She started to clear the dessert plates. "Unfortunately," she said, "your questions have to wait until tomorrow. You two have to go home soon."

The smiles on her friends' faces faded. But Shelly pretended she didn't see. She swam over to place a stack of plates on the kitchen counter.

"I guess Shelly's right," Angel said. "But I wish we didn't have to go."

"Me too," Coral added. "But it's a school night. We can't have a slumber party on a school night."

Shelly swam back to grab more empty plates. "Coral is right," she said. Good thing Coral always wanted to follow the rules.

"I guess we'll see you two tomorrow before sea school?" Angel asked. She and Coral got up from the table.

Every morning, the three kittens met in Leondra's Square and then swam to sea school together. They'd done that all year long. But Shelly suddenly decided something. She could spend more time with Leeza in the morning if they didn't meet up with her friends.

Shelly shook her head. "Leeza and I are going straight to sea school tomorrow," she said. *That way I won't have to share Leeza,* she thought.

"Why?" Coral asked. "We always meet up in the morning."

Shelly bit her lip. She had to think of an excuse quickly. "I want Leeza to have some extra time to get ready," she replied.

"I don't need extra time," Leeza said. "I can be ready whenever you need me to be."

Everyone turned to look at Shelly. She didn't really have a choice. She had to nod. "I guess we will see you in the morning, then," she said. She forced herself to smile.

The other girls didn't notice. Angel, Coral, and Leeza chatted cheerfully for a few more minutes. Then the purrmaids said their goodbyes.

As soon as Shelly shut the door behind her two friends, she felt herself relaxing. She turned back to Leeza and smiled for real. Before she could say anything, Leeza said, "Coral and Angel are really cool. Thank you for making them sit with me."

Shelly frowned. She didn't want to admit that she *hadn't* wanted both of her friends to sit with Leeza. It seemed better to just take credit for the idea. So she said, "I'm glad you liked them. They've been my best friends since we were kittens."

"I hope they liked me, too," Leeza said.

Shelly nodded. But she wanted to stop talking about Angel and Coral! "What do you want to do now?" she asked. "We can play a game. I have Sandy Land, Hungry Hungry Humans—"

"Actually," Leeza interrupted, "it's been a ruff day. I'm tired from the trip. Kittentail Cove is a long way from Dogfish Bay."

"Oh," Shelly said. "So you want to go to bed?"

Leeza nodded and yawned.

Shelly was disappointed. But she tried to hide it. *It makes sense that Leeza is tired,* she thought. "I'll show you where you'll be sleeping," she said.

Shelly helped Leeza get settled on the sofa. "Two pillows and a blanket," she purred. "Do you need anything else?"

"I'm all set," Leeza replied. "I'm just going to listen to some music to fall asleep." She turned a song on.

"What kind of music is that?" Shelly asked. "I've never heard it before."

"It's opera music by Pooch-ini," Leeza said. "My mom loves classical music. So I've learned to like it, too. It's very relaxing."

Shelly nodded. "You're right. Can I listen for a while?"

"Of course!" Leeza said. She lay back on the sofa. Shelly sat on a chair nearby.

When the song was over, Leeza's eyes were almost closed. Shelly tried to float away quietly. But then Leeza whispered, "I'm sorry I'm so sleepy tonight."

Shelly grinned. "Don't worry about it!" she replied. "Sweet dreams. Tomorrow is a big day! You'll get to visit my class at sea school. And we'll have the whole day to get to know each other!"

As Shelly said good night, she really believed that tomorrow would be a fin-tastic day!

4

In the morning, bright and early, Shelly was in the kitchen. She was making her breakfast specialty—scrambled tuna eggs with mango. *I hope Leeza and Chef Atwater will like it!* she thought. She wanted everything to be purr-fect for the grrrmaids' first morning in Kittentail Cove.

Leeza swam to the table just as Shelly was placing the last plate. She was wearing a purr-ty red top decorated with pearls. "Good morning!" she said. "Something smells delicious!"

"I made lots and lots of breakfast," Shelly said. "I hope everyone is hungry!"

"We are!" two voices said at the same time. Shelly's sisters plopped into their seats. Mom, Dad, and Chef Atwater followed soon after.

This time, Shelly made sure Leeza was sitting next to her. "We finally have a chance to talk!" she whispered.

Leeza nodded. She finished chewing and then said, "Shelly, this is delicious!"

Shelly grinned. "Thank you!" she replied. "What do you usually eat for breakfast in Dogfish Bay?"

"My dad's specialty is woofles," Leeza said. Then she whispered, "Don't tell him, but the woofles from Starbarks are better than his!"

Before she could say more, there was a knock at the door. "Who could that be?" Mom asked. She opened the door. "Angel and Coral!" she exclaimed. "What a surprise!"

"Good morning!" Coral said. "Angel and I thought we'd meet Shelly and Leeza here."

"This way, Leeza can have extra time to get ready if she needs it," Angel added.

"Come join us for breakfast," Dad said. "Shelly made a lot of food."

Coral and Angel followed Mom into the kitchen. They dropped their backpacks against the wall and pulled two chairs over to the table.

Normally, Shelly would be happy to get more time with her friends. But she just wanted a little time alone with Leeza! She stuck a bite of food into her mouth so no one could see her frowning.

"I see you made your special scrambled tuna eggs, Shelly," Angel said.

Shelly nodded.

"You are so lucky, Leeza," Coral said. "This is the best breakfast!"

"I know! I'm so grrr-ateful that Shelly did this for us," Leeza said.

Shelly flashed a quick smile and then put more food in her mouth. She didn't feel like talking anymore now that Angel and Coral were there.

That didn't stop the others. Between bites, Angel and Coral had lots of questions for Leeza. When it was finally time to leave for school, Shelly was glad to go.

"Do you have everything you need, Leeza?" Shelly asked.

Leeza grabbed her backpack. "Yes, I do!" she replied. "I brought some special things from home to share with your classmates."

"Show us!" Angel exclaimed.

Leeza shook her head. "You have to wait like everyone else!"

The girls waved goodbye to the grown-ups. "I'll see you all this afternoon," Chef Atwater said. He was going to visit sea school to talk to all the students about grrrmaid life. "I hope you're ready for a grrr-eat presentation! I'm very funny, you know."

"Dad jokes," Leeza whispered. "He only tells dad jokes."

The girls giggled.

On the way to sea school, the purr-maids pointed out some of the important things in their town to Leeza. "There's our library," Coral purred.

"And that's Meow Meadow," Angel said. "There is a family of seahorses who lives under that gazebo."

"That's so cool!" Leeza said.

When they arrived at sea school, Shelly said, "We're here!"

Leeza's eyes widened. "Wow!" she said. "This is a beautiful school."

"We're very lucky," Coral said.

"It's even better inside!" Angel said.

"Let's see if Ms. Harbor is already here," Shelly said. "She's very excited to meet you!"

Shelly led the way to Eel-Twelve. Ms. Harbor had hung a bright banner outside the door to the classroom. It read:

Welcome, Leeza! (Grrrmaids are grrr-eat!)

"That's so sweet," Leeza said. "Now I'm not as nervous about being here."

"You never have to be nervous at sea school!" Shelly said. "Especially not in Eel-Twelve. This is one of the friendliest places in the ocean!"

"Then let's go inside," Leeza said. "I'm ready to make some new friends!"

5

Every time Shelly swam through the door of Eel-Twelve, she felt bubbles of excitement in her tummy. That's because she knew Ms. Harbor always planned lessons that were fin-teresting and fun.

Today, Shelly was more excited than she'd ever been. The students of Eel-Twelve would have a chance to learn about grrrmaids—and Shelly's family had made that possible!

"Welcome, girls!" Ms. Harbor said. She swam over to shake Leeza's paw. "You must be Leeza. I'm so happy that you're here!"

"Everyone has been really nice so far," Leeza said shyly. "I'm so grrr-ateful to you all."

"Everyone in Eel-Twelve will be nice, too," Ms. Harbor replied. She swam over to an empty desk next to Shelly's. "This is where you'll be sitting today, Leeza. I thought you'd like to be near Shelly since you are staying with her family."

Shelly grinned. She'd been hoping Leeza would sit near her. *But right next to me is paw-some!*

"Since you are our special guest, Leeza," Ms. Harbor purred, "we want to show you what sea school is like here in Kittentail Cove. It's not a completely

normal day because we have an assembly
this afternoon."

"My dad is going to speak at the assembly!" Leeza said.

Ms. Harbor nodded. "The rest of the
day, you'll be just another student in
Eel-Twelve."

"Which happens to be the best classroom in the whole school!" Angel said.

"I have a fun project planned for all of you," Ms. Harbor said. "But we have to wait for the whole class."

The girls took their seats as the other students arrived. At first, no one noticed Leeza. Then Adrianna bumped into the extra desk. When she looked at who was sitting there, she gasped. "It's a grrrmaid!" she exclaimed.

Suddenly, everyone turned to look at Leeza. Shelly floated to the grrrmaid's side. "This is Leeza Atwater," she said. "She and her father are visiting Kittentail Cove from their home in Dogfish Bay. She's our guest in class today."

The students all smiled and waved.

"I've never met a grrrmaid before," Baker said, shaking Leeza's paw.

"Me neither," Taylor added. "But I'm glad you're here!"

"Leeza, what is Dogfish Bay like?" Cascade asked.

"Is your school like our school?" Umiko asked.

"And where did you get that outfit?" Adrianna asked. "It's beautiful!"

Ms. Harbor floated over to Leeza. "We have Leeza with us all day," she said. "I'm sure you'll be able to ask lots and lots of questions. We also have an assembly for the whole school. Leeza's father, Chef Atwater, is going to talk to us about life in Dogfish Bay." She smiled. "For now, let's give her a little time to get settled!"

There were some moans and groans, but everyone listened to their teacher. When all the students were seated, Ms. Harbor began the math lesson. Time passed quickly. Before Shelly knew it, the recess bell rang.

"Let's go outside for recess," Ms. Harbor announced.

"Come on, Leeza," Shelly whispered. She took Leeza's paw and led her toward the schoolyard. "There are some special things I want to show you."

"You mean *we* want to show her, right?" Angel purred. She winked. She was just squidding around.

Shelly giggled. "You're right!" Then she pointed to the sea fan fence. "I thought *we* could start over there."

Coral's eyes grew wide. "I know what's over there!"

"Why don't you show Leeza?" Shelly suggested. "After all, you're the one who made the discovery."

The girls swam to the fence. Coral leaned over and pointed to a spiky orange starfish. "That's a basket starfish," she

said. "In Kittentail Cove, they're very rare. I found this one when we were doing a practice scavenger hunt."

"I've seen those before!" Leeza exclaimed. "They're not rare in Dogfish Bay."

"That's really fin-teresting," Angel said. "Are there other things that are different about Dogfish Bay and Kitten-tail Cove?"

"I don't know yet!" Leeza said, laughing. "I'm still learning about Kittentail Cove!"

The purrmaids laughed, too. "Let's teach you more about our town," Shelly said. "There's a game we play here called tag."

"We play tag in Dogfish Bay, too," Leeza said.

"Then you know the rules," Shelly replied. "That's good, because you're IT!"

6

The girls played tag until recess ended. They were tired by the time they got back to their desks. But all four were smiling ear to ear!

Ms. Harbor swam to the front of the classroom. "I have a fun lesson for this afternoon," she said. "We're going to read biographies of important purrmaids soon. Who knows what a biography is?"

Leeza shyly raised her paw. "It's a true

story about a grrrmaid's life." She stopped and looked around. "I guess it can also be about a purrmaid's life."

The students giggled.

"You're right!" Ms. Harbor said. "Biographies can help us learn about someone else. Before we read the biographies of other creatures—purrmaids or grrrmaids—I want you to do your own biography project. You're going to interview each other. This way, you can learn something about one of your classmates."

The students began whispering to each other. Everyone was excited about this idea.

"I made a list of interview questions to help you get started," Ms. Harbor continued. She held out a stack of papers to Shelly. "Can you pass these around to everyone, Shelly?" she asked.

My interview with _____

What is your favorite part of school?

_____

What do you think is the most paw-some
thing in the ocean? _____

What do you think is the scariest thing in
the ocean? _____

Do you have any hobbies? _____

_____

What is your favorite paw-liday? _____

What is your favorite color? _____

Shelly swam around the classroom and
handed out a sheet to each student. Soon,
she reached the far side of the room to
give papers to the Catfish Club.

Ms. Harbor said, "I'd like you all to find a partner. Then you can interview each other."

Leeza and I can be partners! Shelly thought. That would be a paw-some way to get to know her.

But by the time she swam back to ask Leeza if she wanted to work together, it was too late. She heard Angel say, "Let's be partners, Leeza!"

"I think that sounds grrr-eat!" Leeza exclaimed.

"Shelly," Coral purred, "I guess that leaves you and me as partners?"

Shelly nodded. She was disappointed that Leeza wouldn't be her partner. *But it's always wonderful to work with Coral,* a voice inside her head reminded her.

Coral pulled her chair over to Shelly's

desk. "We can take turns answering the questions," she said. "I'll ask you first. What is your favorite part of school?"

"You mean besides being with my best friends?" Shelly replied, giggling. "I think my favorite part of school is . . . music class."

Coral nodded. "That's what I would have guessed about you."

"And what is your favorite part of school?" Shelly asked, while scribbling something on her paper.

"Library time," Coral answered.

"I knew it!" Shelly said. She turned her paper around so Coral could see. "I already wrote *library* down!"

Shelly and Coral quickly finished answering all the questions. Then Shelly said, "Let's see if Angel and Leeza are done, too."

"If they are, we can all hang out," Coral added.

Shelly swam up to Angel's desk. "We're finished with our interviews," she said. "How about you two?"

Leeza turned around to face Shelly. She shook her head. "We're not done yet," she said.

"Can we help?" Shelly asked.

Now Leeza frowned. She looked annoyed. "Can you give us a little more time?"

Shelly's smile faded. "Sure," she said. Leeza turned her back to Shelly.

"I think Leeza is just concentrating on the assignment," Coral whispered. "You get that way, too."

Shelly nodded. Her feelings were still hurt. *But I guess what Coral is saying*

makes sense, she thought. She knew she was very picky about how she wanted to get things done. *Maybe that's something Leeza and I have in common.*

Just as Angel and Leeza put their pencils down, Ms. Harbor raised her paw. When it was quiet, she said, "I'd like everyone to hand in your interviews. When we come back to class, we can share them with each other. But now it's time to go to our special assembly."

Shelly knew the rules for assemblies. You sat in the same order as you were lined up. That's why she told Leeza to follow her. "Let me just grrr-ab my backpack," Leeza said.

Shelly didn't know why Leeza needed her bag. But she was too busy making sure she was first in line to worry about that. She also made sure Leeza was right behind her. *Finally,* she thought, *I'll get to sit next to her!*

Coral and Angel lined up behind Leeza.

"You'll be surrounded by friends, Leeza," Shelly whispered.

Leeza grinned. "Thank you for thinking of that!"

"That's what a friend would do!" Shelly exclaimed.

7

When there was an assembly at sea school, everyone gathered in the paw-ditorium. There were enough clamshell seats for all the students. Ms. Harbor's class swam in, single file. The teacher pointed to an empty row in the front of the room. "Please fill in the seats here," she purred. "Sit down quickly and stay in order. That way, Chef Atwater can start on time."

Shelly swam to the far end of the row and sat down. Leeza sat next to her. Coral took the third seat, and Angel took the fourth one. The other students of Eel-Twelve filled in the rest of the row.

"It's nice to be with you," Shelly said to Leeza. "It feels like we haven't had a minute all day."

Leeza nodded. But she wasn't smiling like she was before. In fact, she wasn't really paying attention. She was looking all around for someone. Shelly wasn't sure what was going on.

When Ms. Harbor swam past, Leeza grabbed her bag and popped out of her seat. She darted over to Ms. Harbor and whispered something. The teacher listened and nodded. She swam to Taylor and said something to him. Then Taylor got out of his seat. Leeza took his place.

Taylor swam to Leeza's old seat and sat down. He was frowning.

"What happened?" Shelly asked.

Taylor shrugged. "I don't know," he muttered. "The new girl said something to Ms. Harbor who made me switch places." He crossed his paws. "Now I don't get to sit next to Baker."

Shelly began to think about the other things that had happened. Leeza wanted to talk at dinner when Coral and Angel were there. But as soon as they left, she was too tired to talk anymore. Leeza was happy to play tag when Angel and Coral were also playing. But she didn't wait to be Shelly's partner for the project. And she didn't want to sit with Shelly at the assembly. The moment she could, Leeza asked Ms. Harbor to change her seat.

Shelly felt her face getting hot. *Leeza doesn't want to be friends with* me!

It felt like there were butterfly fish darting around in Shelly's tummy. But it wasn't because she was excited. Shelly felt so bad about Leeza that her tummy started to hurt.

Shelly glanced over at Coral and Angel. They were whispering to each other. At

the end of the row, Leeza was looking through her backpack. None of them even looked in Shelly's direction.

Shelly could feel tears welling in her eyes. She didn't want anyone to see. She darted over to Ms. Harbor and tapped her on the shoulder. "Excuse me," she said. "I don't feel well. Can I go to the nurse?"

"What's going on?" Ms. Harbor asked.

Shelly put a paw on her belly. "This hurts," she replied. That was true.

"That's not good," Ms. Harbor said. "Get to the nurse's office and see what she says. I hope you feel better soon."

Shelly nodded and swam out of the paw-ditorium. She wanted to get away from everyone in Eel-Twelve.

Mrs. Wells was the school nurse. She had Shelly lie down. "You don't have a fever, Shelly," she purred. "Are you sure you don't want to go back to the assembly?"

Shelly shook her head.

"Do you want me to call your parents?" Mrs. Wells asked.

Shelly nodded. "Yes, please."

"I'll bet you'll feel better after you rest at home," Mrs. Wells said as she picked up her shell phone.

Shelly said, "Thank you, Mrs. Wells." She turned to face the wall and closed her eyes. That didn't stop a few tears from falling. *Nothing about this day is turning out the way I wanted,* she thought.

8

Even though it was a very busy day for the Lake Restaurant, Mom came to sea school as soon as she could. Shelly heard her talking to Mrs. Wells. "She has a tummy ache," Mrs. Wells said.

Mom gently touched Shelly's shoulder. "Wake up, Shelly," she whispered. "I'm here to take you home." She was already carrying Shelly's backpack.

Shelly got up slowly. She waved good-bye to Mrs. Wells. Then she and Mom swam out of sea school.

"How are you feeling now, Shelly?" Mom asked when they got home. "Should I call the doctor's office?"

Shelly bit her lip. She had to be honest with Mom. She didn't want her family to worry for no reason. "Mom," she said, "I have to tell you something. I don't think I'm sick."

"Then what's going on?" Mom asked. "You don't look like yourself. What's wrong?"

Shelly took a deep breath. "It was such a terrible day. I thought Leeza and I would become friends today. I really wanted her to like me. But she doesn't like me!"

"I don't think that's true," Mom

purred. "Chef Atwater was just telling me how excited his daughter was to be here with you."

Shelly shook her head. "Leeza likes Angel and Coral. But she had Ms. Harbor change her seat at the assembly just because she was sitting next to me!"

"Is that what she said?" Mom asked.

"I didn't ask," Shelly replied. "I just felt awful when she did that." She looked down at her tail. "I'm sorry I pretended to be sick. I just really needed to come home."

Mom pulled Shelly into a big hug. "Just because you may not have an illness doesn't mean you were pretending. It sounds like your heart is hurting right now."

Shelly nodded.

"Being healthy isn't just about your

body," Mom said. "It's about your thoughts and feelings, too. If your heart is feeling sick, you need to figure out how to make it feel better." She gave Shelly a squeeze. "But we'll keep an eye on that tummy anyway, just in case."

"Thank you, Mom," Shelly whispered.

"Do you want to come to the restaurant with me?" Mom asked. "We have to get ready for the feast tonight."

Shelly shook her head. "I don't want to see anyone right now."

Mom kissed the top of Shelly's head. "I can understand that," she said. "Your sisters are going to go straight to the restaurant after school, so you'll have the whole house to yourself. If you change your mind, you know where to find me."

Shelly plopped down on her oyster bed. Everything went wrong today. Leeza didn't want to be her friend. Angel and Coral—who were supposed to be Shelly's best friends—hadn't noticed. She felt so alone.

Shelly closed her eyes. There was a part

of her that wanted to go to sleep and wake up tomorrow. But she couldn't sleep. She just tossed and turned and felt sadder and sadder.

Suddenly, Shelly heard a knock at the door.

"Shelly?" called a voice.

"Are you here?" added another voice.

It's Coral and Angel, Shelly thought. She sighed. She really didn't want to talk to anyone. *But they came all the way here to check on me. I can't ignore them.*

The purrmaids outside knocked again. "I'm coming," Shelly shouted. She floated over to let her friends in.

"Are you all right, Shelly?" Coral asked immediately.

"You left so quickly," Angel purred. "We were worried about you."

Shelly looked down at her tail. "I wasn't feeling well," she said. "I wanted to come home."

"You missed the assembly," Coral said.

Shelly shrugged.

"And you missed hearing all the class interviews," Angel said.

Shelly shrugged again.

Angel and Coral looked at each other. Then Coral put a paw on Shelly's shoulder. "Is there something we can do to make you feel better?"

Shelly felt teardrops run down her cheeks. Angel and Coral rushed forward to hug her.

"Don't cry, Shelly," Angel whispered. "We're here to help you."

"Today made me feel so bad," Shelly said. "I wanted to make it a purr-fect day for Leeza. But I think she'd enjoy her stay in Kittentail Cove without me."

Both of Shelly's friends frowned. "Why do you think that?" Coral asked.

"Because she's tried to get away from me since last night!" Shelly exclaimed. "I don't know why she decided she doesn't like me. But we'll never be friends."

Angel and Coral looked at each other

again. Coral nodded, and Angel held out two pieces of paper. "Look, Shelly," Coral said. "These are the interviews that Angel and I did."

"We looked at your answers and Leeza's

Coral

My interview with _Shelly_

What is your favorite part of school?
music class

What do you think is the most paw-some thing in the ocean? _sea turtles_

What do you think is the scariest thing in the ocean? _giant octopuses_

Do you have any hobbies? _making new recipes_

What is your favorite paw-liday? _Fish-mas_

What is your favorite color? _pink_

answers," Angel said. "We noticed some-thing fin-teresting."

Shelly looked at the pages. Then her eyes grew wide. "We gave almost the same answers!"

Angel

My interview with Leeza

What is your favorite part of school?
Music lessons

What do you think is the most paw-some thing in the ocean? Sea turtles

What do you think is the scariest thing in the ocean? Any kind of octopus

Do you have any hobbies? Thinking of new recipes

What is your favorite paw-liday? Fish-mas

What is your favorite color? Pink

9

Shelly kept staring at the interview pages. She couldn't believe that Leeza's answers were so much like her own.

"You two have a lot in common," Coral said.

"We didn't know if you realized that," Angel said.

Shelly shook her head. "I didn't know. I thought Leeza and I were as different as jellyfish and humans!" She frowned. "But then why doesn't she like me?" she asked.

"Have you talked to her about how you feel?" Angel asked.

Shelly shook her head.

"You know," Coral purred, "it's really hard to guess how someone else is feeling. Especially when you're still trying to get to know each other."

"Leeza was looking for you at the assembly," Angel added. "She called for you from the stage."

"Why?" Shelly asked.

Angel replied, "We don't know. You weren't there, so they moved to a new topic."

"Afterward," Coral said, "when we found out you went to the nurse, she was worried about you, too."

Shelly scratched her head. "Do you think Leeza thinks I left early because I didn't care about the Dogfish Bay assembly?"

Angel and Coral both shrugged. "Maybe," Angel said.

Shelly frowned even harder. *I've been so busy thinking of the ways my feelings got hurt,* she thought, *I haven't thought about what Leeza might be thinking. What if we are both misunderstanding each other?*

"I think it's time that I talk to Leeza," Shelly said. "Do you know where she went after school?"

"Her dad was still at sea school when the day ended," Coral replied. "She's probably with him."

"Then I know where to go," Shelly said.

"We'll come with you," Angel said. "That's what friends are for!"

The purrmaids swam to the Lake Restaurant. They saw Leeza through the window. She was sitting alone at one of the tables. Her backpack was on the ground next to her.

"I should go talk to her by myself," Shelly said.

"We'll be right here if you need us," Angel said.

"You don't have to stay," Shelly answered. "I don't know how long this will take."

"It doesn't matter," Coral purred. "Take your time. We'll wait."

Shelly hugged her friends before swimming into the restaurant. Leeza didn't look up from the book she was reading.

Shelly gently tapped Leeza's shoulder. "Excuse me," she purred.

Leeza turned around. "Shelly," she said. "I didn't know you were here."

"I came looking for you," Shelly said.

"Why?" Leeza asked.

Shelly took a deep breath. "I wanted to apologize. I left the assembly today because I thought you didn't like me. At least not as much as you like Angel and Coral."

"What are you talking about?" Leeza asked.

Shelly looked away. "You seemed to get along with them just fine. But you didn't want to hang out with me last night."

"I was tired!" Leeza exclaimed. "I really was. I would've talked to you all night. But I couldn't keep my eyes open. Besides, I thought *you* didn't like me!

I thought you kept sending them to be with me because *you* didn't want to be with me!"

"But you had Ms. Harbor change your seat at the assembly," Shelly said. "I thought you wanted to sit next to anyone but me."

"That's not true!" Leeza said. "My dad said he was going to have me join him during the assembly. I wanted to sit on the end so I'd be close to the stage when he did." Leeza reached for Shelly's paw. "I've been looking forward to meeting you for ages!"

"Me too!" Shelly said. "I guess I should have talked to you more, instead of just deciding that I knew what you were feeling."

"I should have done that, too," Leeza said.

"It's hard when you're trying to make a new friend," Shelly said. "You get nervous when you don't need to be nervous."

"And you worry about things you don't need to worry about," Leeza said.

The girls looked at each other and smiled.

"Maybe we could start again," Shelly purred. "I'm Shelly, and I'm really excited to meet you. I hope we can be friends." She held out her paw.

Leeza shook Shelly's paw and said, "I'm Leeza, and I ruff-use to let anything get in the way of our friendship!"

10

Leeza leaned over and grabbed her bag. She leafed through it. "You left before the assembly. You didn't get to see the things we brought from Dogfish Bay."

Leeza took out a stack of photos. "This is my family's restaurant," she said, handing the picture to Shelly. "And this is a photo of my school."

"It looks a lot like sea school!" Shelly exclaimed.

Leeza nodded. "We have a park in our town that's a lot like Meow Meadow," she continued. She handed Shelly another photo. "Meow Meadow is a grrr-den of corals and sea grass. But our park, Pup-land Place, is a field of seashells." She grabbed a pawful of shells from her bag and passed them to Shelly. "There are lots of scallop shells, shark's eye shells, and slipper shells. There are some very rare shells, too." Leeza reached into her bag one more time. Then she held out three tiny, beautiful shells. "These are called kittenpaw shells. I thought since you're a purrmaid, you mutt really like these. I brought them for you as a gift. I was going to give them to you on stage in front of everyone."

Shelly put the other shells down. She took one of the kittenpaw shells from

Leeza. It was a white shell with little ridges that made it look just like a purrmaid's paw.

Leeza said, "I know every time I see a kittenpaw shell back home, I'll think about my purrmaid friends. And maybe, every time you see these shells, you'll think of me." She handed over the other two shells.

Shelly gave Leeza a big hug. Then she said, "I can't keep these."

Leeza frowned. "You don't like them?"

"I do like them!" Shelly replied. "I just mean, I can't keep all three of these. After all, I'm not your only purrmaid friend." She winked. "If it's all right with you, I'll keep one shell and you can give the other two to Angel and Coral—your other purrmaid friends."

Leeza's frown disappeared and she smiled at Shelly. "That is a paw-some idea!"

Shelly grabbed Leeza's paw. "Come on!" she said. "Let's go find them!"

Coral and Angel were floating right around the corner from the restaurant. Shelly grinned when she spotted them. *My friends never leave me alone when I need them*, she thought.

Shelly pulled Leeza toward her friends. "Angel! Coral!" she called.

"Did you two work things out?" Coral asked.

Shelly and Leeza smiled at each other. "We talked everything through," Leeza said.

"There were a lot of misunderstandings," Shelly added. "The three of us have been friends fur-ever. It's easy to be friends with you. So I forgot that it can be hard to make a new friend."

"It might be hard," Angel said, "but it's worth it when you get a paw-some friend like Shelly."

"I a-grrr-ee!" Leeza said.

Shelly gently elbowed Leeza. "Is there something you wanted to show Coral and Angel?"

Leeza's eyes widened. "There is!" She reached into her bag again and took out two kittenpaw shells. "I brought these from Dogfish Bay. They remind me of purrmaids. Shelly suggested I give one to each of my purrmaid friends." She smiled. "Do you like them?"

"These are beautiful!" Angel said.

"We can add them to our friendship bracelets!" Coral added.

"That way we'll remember your visit

every time we see them, Leeza," Shelly purred.

Each of the purrmaids gave Leeza a hug to say thank you. Then Leeza said, "Everything worked out purr-fectly."

But Shelly shook her head. "Not yet."

"What do you mean?" Coral asked.

Shelly grinned. "We still have a feast to get to!" she exclaimed.

There was already a crowd forming at the front door of the Lake Restaurant. So Shelly led her friends to the back entrance. They swam in and found Mom in the kitchen.

"Girls," Mom said. "I wasn't sure if you'd come for dinner tonight."

"I'd like a table for four." Shelly winked at Leeza. "Something grrr-eat, please!"

"We're purr-ty busy," Mom replied. But then she winked, too. "It's a good thing you girls know someone with connections." She waved for them to follow. "I have a fin-tastic table for you."

Mom led the girls to their seats. Leeza made sure to sit next to Shelly. "No misunderstandings this time," she whispered. "*Bone* appétit!" she said to everyone. "That means I hope you enjoy the food!"

"Since I missed your father's assembly," Shelly said, "you'll have to explain the things he's cooking."

Leeza smiled. "Of course I will," she said. "What are friends for?"

The purrmaids have lots of friends around the ocean!

Read on for a peek at this adventure about their mermicorn friends!

The first time the girls met, Lily wasn't sure if she and Sirena were going to be friends. Even when they became partners in Ms. Trainor's class, things were a bit stormy. But then they got stuck in Barracuda Belt during a *real* storm. They helped each other and, like magic, their friendship began.

Sirena lived between Lily's house and the Magic Academy. That was one reason the girls decided to meet outside the

Chevals' house before school in the morning. They could swim together the rest of the way.

The other reason to meet at Sirena's house was her oyster garden. On their first day at the Magic Academy, Sirena had given Lily a silver necklace. They agreed that every time they learned a new bit of mermicorn magic, they would add a pearl to their necklaces.

The first magical skill that Ms. Trainor taught the class was how to make their horns glow. It didn't seem very exciting at first. But it came in handy during that storm! Lily and Sirena had been practicing that magic every chance they got. They finally felt like they'd really learned it. Today was the day they would pick out their first pearls.

Lily swam up to the Chevals' house. Mrs. Cheval opened the door.

"Good morning, Mrs. Cheval," Lily said.

"Good morning, Lily," Mrs. Cheval replied. "Come on in. Sirena will be ready in a minute."

"I'm just finishing a sea mail," Sirena called from the other room.

"Are you ready for your first pearl,

Lily?" Mrs. Cheval asked.
"Show me what you've
learned."

Lily took a deep breath.
She closed her eyes and
found her sparkle. Then
she said, "Pickle tree,
manatee, let there be . . .
light!" The twinkles soon
became a bright glow. "I did
it!" Lily exclaimed. "It was
easy peasy, turtle squeezy!"

"That was great!" Mrs. Cheval
neighed. "And as you get better at magic,
you won't even have to say the magic
words out loud."

"But they're so much fun to say!"
Sirena said as she swam into the room.

"Are you finally ready, Sirena?" Lily

asked. She winked so her friend would know she was just squidding around.

Sirena nodded. "Let's go pick out our pearls!"

The mermicorns floated to the oyster garden. The girls were so excited that they picked the first oysters they saw. They carefully opened the shells.

"My pearl is blue!" Sirena said.

"And mine is yellow!" Lily added.

Mrs. Cheval helped the fillies put the pearls on their necklaces. "Beautiful," she said. "Now you'd better get to school. I want you each to earn your next pearl!"

Sirena kissed her mother's cheek. "Hey, Mom," she said, "is it still fine for us to go to that clubhouse I found?"

Mrs. Cheval nodded.

Lily raised her eyebrows. *What is Sirena talking about?*